Dedication

This book is dedicated to my grandchildren and to grandparents who take time to create treasured memories with their grandchildren.

Acknowledgments

Thank you to all my family, friends, and colleagues who supported me in this endeavor.

. . . .

There are many memories we keep for a lifetime. I want to create memories my grandchildren will keep beyond their lifetime.

Published by Tate Publishing & Enterprises, LLC
127 E. Trade Center Terrace | Mustang, Oklahoma 73064 USA
1.888.361.9473 | www.tatepublishing.com

Tate Publishing is committed to excellence in the publishing industry. The company reflects the philosophy established by the founders, based on Psalm 68:11,
"The Lord gave the word and great was the company of those who published it."

Published in the United States of America

ISBN: 978-1-61862-633-2
1. Juvenile Fiction / Family / Multigenerational
2. Juvenile Fiction / General
12.02.29

The Grandma Box

written by Debbie Brown

tate publishing
CHILDREN'S DIVISION

"Hi, my name is Nicole."

"Hi, my name is Caitlin."

"We love our Grandma Box."

"Grandma is coming to visit. We can't wait for her to come; she always brings the Grandma Box."

The Grandma Box is filled with fun things to play with. There are many small boxes inside the Grandma Box. There is something special in each little box. Nicole likes that the things inside, are always the same, in neat little boxes. Nicole likes to keep things neat and organized. Caitlin likes that sometimes there are new surprises in the little boxes. Caitlin likes surprises.

We like to find a quiet place to play with the Grandma Box. Mommy and Daddy can't play with the Grandma Box; it's only for Grandma and us. When Mommy and Daddy try to peek, we hide it!

It's an adventure when we pick Grandma up at the noisy train station. When Grandma steps off the train, we jump up and down because we're so excited. We know the Grandma Box is in her big red suitcase.

9

One fun afternoon, we took the Grandma Box to the park. Grandma helped us throw the big, white parachutes high into the air, and we watched them float to the ground.

When we went camping in the mountains with Grandma, we had fun rolling the cars from the Grandma Box down a huge boulder. Then we played catch with the balls under the tall, smelly pine trees.

Another time we sat in the car with Grandma while mommy was shopping. It was raining really hard outside. We were glad we had the Grandma Box. We blew bubbles and played "Go Fish." Caitlin won every time.

Once on a warm sunny day, we sat on Grandma's old quilt in the salty air. We laughed while we covered ourselves with sand and ran away from the crashing waves. When it was time to leave, we almost forgot the toy dog we had buried in the sand!

Maybe next time we visit Grandma at her house, we can sit on the lawn under the big, swaying, willow tree again. It's fun looking at all the red ladybugs, slimy snails, and wiggly worms with the magnifying glass.

We miss Grandma when she leaves. Sometimes she lets us pick something from the Grandma Box to keep until she comes back. We keep it in a safe place and take good care of it until she visits again.

When we play with the Grandma Box, we talk about many things. Grandma listens to what we have to say and plays with us. We can tell Grandma loves us because she spends time with just us. "We love our grandma."

"She's here! She's here!"

"Let's go help Grandma carry in the Grandma Box."

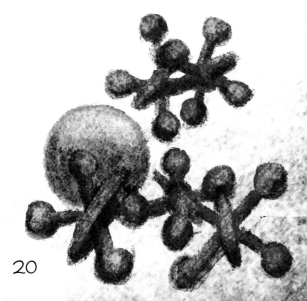

Things in Our Grandma Box

1. marbles

2. cars

3. snowmen

4. seashells

5. coins

6. balls

7. music box

8. bubbles

9. felt pens

10. bowling pins

11. a toy dog

12. a butterfly that guards the key to the coin box

13. magnifying glass

14. bugs

15. jacks

16. lavender

17. parachutes

What would You Put in Your Grandma Box?

_____

_____

_____

_____

_____

_____

_____

Where do you think the Grandma
Box will be many years from now?

_____

_____

Where else could you take
the Grandma Box?

_____

_____

_____

_____

# e|LIVE

---

listen|imagine|view|experience

AUDIO BOOK DOWNLOAD INCLUDED WITH THIS BOOK!

In your hands you hold a complete digital entertainment package. In addition to the paper version, you receive a free download of the audio version of this book. Simply use the code listed below when visiting our website. Once downloaded to your computer, you can listen to the book through your computer's speakers, burn it to an audio CD or save the file to your portable music device (such as Apple's popular iPod) and listen on the go!

How to get your free audio book digital download:

1. Visit www.tatepublishing.com and click on the e|LIVE logo on the home page.
2. Enter the following coupon code:
   ab93-53ab-0fc2-f4c0-d994-0ca5-c454-fc04
3. Download the audio book from your e|LIVE digital locker and begin enjoying your new digital entertainment package today!